For Joyce
—J.S.

To my family and friends
—B.T.

This version of an ancient Native American myth typifies the stories told by many of the nations who once inhabited the Great Plains and western United States. Passed on by word of mouth and rarely written down, these tales often incorporated animals as heroes and tricksters. The coyote, indigenous to that part of the country, was admired for his slyness and resourcefulness.

Although the essence of this story can be traced to one probably of Crow origin, cited in *Legends of the United Nations* by Frances Frost (New York: Whittlesey House, 1943), I have drawn on other tales of the coyote as creator. These include *Don Coyote* by Leigh Peck (Boston: Houghton Mifflin, 1942); *Index to Fairy Tales, Myths & Legends: Second Supplement* by Mary House Eastman (Boston: F. W. Faxon Co., 1952); and "Old Man Coyote Makes the World" from *American Indian Myths and Legends* edited by Erdoes and Ortiz (New York: Pantheon, 1984).

In many of these tales, the coyote and other animals have already been created by the spirits. Then, acting as a conduit for these same spirits, coyote, often with the help of others, takes on the final delicate task of making man. Interestingly, most of these tales do not account for the separate creation of woman.

Coyote Makes Man is essentially a myth that, like a map, serves as a guide to the unknown. I hope that this tale will inspire young readers to explore the richness of Native American mythology and culture.

SIMON & SCHUSTER BOOKS FOR YOUNG READERS
An imprint of Simon & Schuster Children's Publishing Division
1230 Avenue of the Americas, New York, New York 10020
Text copyright © 1994 by James Sage. Illustrations copyright © 1994 by Britta Teckentrup.
All rights reserved including the right of reproduction in whole or in part in any form.
Originally published in Great Britain by ABC, All Books for Children,
a division of The All Children's Company Ltd. First American Edition, 1995.
SIMON & SCHUSTER BOOKS FOR YOUNG READERS is a trademark of Simon & Schuster.
Book design by Paul Zakris. The text for this book is set in 16-point Berkeley Black.
The illustrations were done in oil paints on newsprint—with roler and
monoprint techniques—followed by collage on paper.
Manufactured in Singapore
10 9 8 7 6 5 4 3 2 1
Library of Congress Catalog Card Number: 94-67687
ISBN: 0-689-80011-8

Coyote Makes Man

BY
James Sage

ILLUSTRATED BY
Britta Teckentrup

Simon & Schuster
Books for Young Readers

It was Coyote who put the final touches on the earth. When he had finished scooping out the lakes, and heaping up the mountains, and had rolled out the tree-covered hills, and made the grass grow tall on the prairies, and had filled the streams and riverbeds with cool, clean water, he called a meeting of the animals.

They gathered in a forest clearing, and Coyote said to them, "I have asked you here to discuss my final creation—Man. What should he be like?"

"He must be able to walk on all fours or stand upright when he chooses," said Bear without hesitation. "And he must have a thick, woolly coat to keep him warm in the winter."

"No, no!" said Deer. "He should have antlers to defend himself and be able to run like the wind."

Fox shook his head. "Man must have cunning and a beautiful, bushy tail to wrap around himself at night."

"Who says?" hooted Owl. "It is much more important to see clearly in the dark and have good hearing."

"Nonsense," scoffed Otter. "It is only necessary that Man swim to perfection and have an excellent sense of humor."

"Excuse me," muttered Beaver, "but what Man really needs is a set of sharp teeth for gnawing through tree trunks and a broad tail to slap on the water as a danger signal."

"Perhaps," honked Snow Goose, "but he must also have strong wings when it comes time to fly south."

"And what about fishing?" argued
Pelican. "Where would Man be without
a beak? How would he be able to catch
his dinner?"

Their voices grew louder and louder until Coyote could stand it no longer. "Quiet!" he commanded. "We have yet to hear from Field Mouse. What does he have to say?"

"Well," said Field Mouse nervously, "I think Man should have large ears and long, tweeky whiskers and a good nose for smelling. And that is all he needs. I think."

The other animals laughed at the thought of Man looking like a Field Mouse!

"Enough!" said Coyote. "Show me your idea of Man." And he gave them each a lump of clay. The animals worked until the sun dropped low in the sky and long shadows appeared on the ground.

"We can continue in the morning," said Coyote. "Let us rest now."

When Coyote saw that all the animals were asleep, he looked at their models. Each animal had made Man in his own image.

"This will never do," said Coyote, and he poured water over the models until they were lumps of clay again. Then, with great care, he began to shape his own image of Man.

He gave him eyes that he might see, and ears that he might hear, and teeth for biting and chewing. He gave Man legs for running, and arms for swinging, and fingers for holding and touching. He gave him hair for warmth, and a nose for smelling, and a voice to speak and sing with, and a heart for courage, and a brain so that he might acquire wisdom and be at peace with all things.

Last of all, he gave Man the precious gift of Life, without which everything else was meaningless.

Man stirred and opened his eyes. He gazed at the beautiful world and smiled.

As the sun rose, the animals awakened.

They yawned and stretched and looked around. The clay models were gone, and in their place was a creature who combined the best of all their features.

The animals were impressed with Coyote's achievement.

"Now the world is perfect," they said.

Only Coyote wasn't so sure.